Happy Birthday, Caroline?

"Since your birthdays are just fifteen days apart," Mrs. Zucker said to Caroline and Vicki, "your father and I have decided to have one big party for both of you."

Caroline couldn't believe her ears. *One party?* A party with Vicki and all her six-year-old friends? She scrunched her eyes shut, hoping that maybe she was dreaming. But when she opened them again, she knew it wasn't a bad dream.

"My friends are all *nine,*" she cried. "They're going to *hate* coming to a party with Vicki and her friends. Everyone at school is going to laugh when they hear about my stupid party with the kindergarteners!"

Caroline bit her lower lip. Her nose was itchy and there were hot tears behind her eyes. This was going to be the biggest disaster that had ever happened!

Look for these books in the Caroline Zucker series:

Caroline Zucker
And The Birthday Disaster

by Jan Bradford

Illustrated by Marcy Ramsey

Troll Associates

Library of Congress Cataloging-in-Publication Data

Bradford, Jan.
  Caroline Zucker and the birthday disaster / by Jan Bradford;
illustrated by Marcy Ramsey.
     p.   cm.
  Summary: Eight-year-old Caroline Zucker is upset when she learns
that she and her youngest sister Vicki must share a birthday party.
  ISBN 0-8167-2021-5 (lib. bdg.)   ISBN 0-8167-2022-3 (pbk.)
  [1. Birthdays—Fiction. 2. Sisters—Fiction. 3. Friendship—
Fiction.] I. Ramsey, Marcy Dunn, ill. II. Title.
PZ7.B7228Cap 1991
[Fic]—dc20   90-11159

A TROLL BOOK, published by Troll Associates,
Mahwah, NJ 07430

Printed in the United States of America.
10 9 8 7 6 5 4 3 2 1

1

ALMOST NINE!

"Will your Grandpa really give us candy?" Maria Santiago asked. She and her best friend, Caroline Zucker, were riding their bikes on the sidewalk. They had stopped at a red light one block before Grandpa Nevelson's candy store.

"Sure. Why do you always ask me?" Caroline's grandfather never turned them down.

The light changed and Maria crossed the street. Caroline followed her, admiring her best friend's new green bike. Maria had gotten it for her ninth birthday, and Caroline wanted one just like it in red or blue for her own ninth birthday in less than two weeks.

Maria pointed to a girl they were passing. She was walking along, listening to a pink radio-cassette player. Maria called over her shoulder to Caroline, "Isn't that neat?"

"I think I'll put it on my birthday list," Caroline yelled. "I can play my new Lucy Hanson tape on it."

Maria stopped so Caroline could catch up with her. "I didn't know you had Lucy's new tape."

"I don't—yet." Caroline grinned. "But I'm hoping I'll get it for my birthday."

They pedaled past Benny's Video and the drug store to Nevelson's Candy Shoppe. After they parked their bikes in the rack and locked Caroline's chain around both of them, they went into the store.

"If it's not Caroline Louise and her charming friend, the lovely Maria!" Grandpa Nevelson boomed from behind the counter.

People turned to see if anyone really famous had come into the store. When they saw it was only two little girls, they went back to their shopping. But Caroline's face turned pink anyway.

"Why does he *always* do that?" Maria asked. Her cheeks were pink, too.

2

Caroline said, "I guess he just likes us."

"What can I do for you, girls?" Caroline's grandfather asked when he finished helping a customer.

"Something to eat!" Caroline grabbed her stomach. "We're *starving*!"

Grandpa Nevelson shook his head sadly, but his eyes were twinkling. "All I have is candy. Will that do?"

"Yes, sir," Maria said.

"Sir!" He reached over the counter to ruffle her black, wavy hair. "No one—and I mean absolutely *no one*—calls me 'sir.' Just pretend I'm your grandpa, too."

"All right, Grandpa—sir," Maria said shyly.

Caroline understood Maria's problem. Mrs. Santiago always insisted that Maria be respectful to adults. "We're still starving, Grandpa," Caroline reminded the white-haired man.

"And I bet you need some energy to get home in time for dinner," he teased.

Maria and Caroline both nodded.

"You can each pick two treats," he told them. "On the house."

"Thanks, Grandpa!" Caroline hurried over to the candy counter. She ignored the kids who were staring at her with open mouths. Whenever Grandpa Nevelson let Caroline or her sisters have free candy, other kids always got jealous.

"I'm going to get a chocolate bar and a big sucker," she said to Maria. "What about you?"

"Peppermints and a bag of peanuts," her friend answered. Then she added, "Thank you, Grandpa, sir."

With their snacks in hand, the girls sneaked into the office at the back of the store, though they didn't really need to. Grandpa Nevelson always let them eat their candy back there.

Caroline sat in her grandfather's old-fashioned wooden chair with the wheels on the bottom. Then she put her feet on his desktop and ripped the wrapper off her chocolate bar.

Maria sat down in a chair next to the desk. "What kind of party are you having for your birthday?" she asked.

Caroline shrugged. "I don't know yet."

"But it's real soon, isn't it?" Maria popped a peppermint into her mouth.

Inside her head, Caroline counted. "Ten more days," she said.

"And you don't have any party plans?" Maria sounded shocked.

"No . . ." Now that she thought about it, Caroline realized it was strange. People had to be invited, and her mother would have to bake a cake. "My folks haven't said anything."

Maria's dark eyes got big. "Do you think they forgot?"

"Forgot that I'm having a birthday?" Caroline knew that would be impossible. Parents never forgot things like that—did they? Besides, hers wasn't the only birthday coming up in the Zucker family. Caroline's little sister Vicki would be six just two weeks after Caroline turned nine. What mother or dad could forget *two* birthdays?

Maria frowned. "Maybe they're too busy to think about it," she said. Then she had a great idea. "If your folks aren't going to plan your party, then *we* can!"

"Roller skating at Skate World?" Caroline suggested eagerly. Their school had a party at Skate World once a year, and she loved it.

"That would be fun!" Maria ate another peppermint. "Or how about a makeover party? We could all fix our hair and our nails and try putting on makeup."

Caroline's brown eyes sparkled. "Oh, yes!"

6

"My mother lets me try her blush on my cheeks sometimes," Maria said.

"How does it look?" Caroline touched her hand to her own cheek.

Maria giggled. "Better than *you* look with chocolate all over your face!"

Caroline checked her fingers. They were covered with melted chocolate. Grinning, she grabbed a handful of tissues from the box on her grandfather's desk and scrubbed her cheeks. "Am I okay now?"

Maria leaned closer to get a good look. "Yes. Now you look like I do when I wear my mom's blush. It makes my cheeks all red, just like I'd been rubbing them!"

"Well, my mom squirted some of her perfume on my neck before she went to dinner with my dad last week," Caroline said.

"Did it smell good? Like flowers?"

Caroline's nose wrinkled. "No, it was kind of spicy. And it made my nose itch!"

"Do you think your mother would help us with a makeover party?" Maria asked.

"I don't know . . . like you said, she's been awfully busy lately. Maybe we should come up with another idea." Caroline closed her eyes and thought hard. "I know! A sleepover with scary movies!"

"That would be easy." Maria liked the idea, too. "You could rent some videos and buy a bunch of snacks at the store."

"Why are you going to buy snacks?" Grandpa Nevelson asked as he came into the office.

His booming voice made Caroline jump. She took her feet off his desk. "We were talking about party snacks . . . chips and caramel corn and soda. . . ."

Grandpa Nevelson pretended to be confused. "Who's having a party?"

"Me!" Caroline cried. "I hope."

"And is there some reason for this party?" he asked.

Caroline knew he was teasing. "I'm having a birthday!"

"Oh, that's right. You're going to be . . ."

"Nine!" Caroline told him, wondering if he really couldn't remember.

Grandpa Nevelson shook his head. "That's pretty old," he said solemnly.

Maria smiled at him. "I'm nine."

"I should have known. You look much older than my granddaughter."

"Grandpa! Maria's only a few months older

8

than me!" Caroline hopped out of the chair and stood as tall as she could. "I'm not a baby anymore!"

He studied her and rubbed his chin. Then he glanced at Maria. "I guess you're not, Caroline Louise. You know, being nine is very special."

"What's so special about it?" Maria asked. She was interested because she was already nine.

Grandpa Nevelson had a twinkle in his eye. "That's for me to know and for you girls to find out!"

2

PARENTS CAN'T CANCEL BIRTHDAYS—CAN THEY?

"I win," Caroline announced as she twisted the water out of her dishrag. Since they had to wash the dinner dishes by hand, she'd decided it would be more fun if they pretended it was a race.

Her almost-seven-year-old sister Patricia frowned. She grabbed the frying pan and hurried to dry it with her towel. "You're not playing fair. You started before me."

Vicki, the youngest and the shortest Zucker, climbed on a chair to reach the counter better. One by one, she picked up the plates Patricia had dried and put them into the cupboard.

Patricia brushed her blond hair out of her face. "When are Mom and Dad going to get the dishwasher fixed?"

"I don't know, but I hope it's soon," Caroline said as she sponged the water off the counter. If they left the kitchen very clean, maybe their mother would let her call Maria. She needed to make more birthday plans with her best friend.

Mrs. Zucker came into the kitchen. "It's looking good in here, ladies."

Caroline smiled. "Thanks, Mom. Now can I use the phone?"

"In a minute," Mrs. Zucker said. "First I need to talk to you and Vicki."

"What about me?" asked Patricia, pouting.

"Sure. Let's all go into the family room." Their mother helped Vicki climb off the chair. Then all four of them went into the cozy room behind the kitchen. Baxter, the Zuckers' big, shaggy dog, followed them.

Caroline sat at one end of the couch, Patricia curled her legs beneath her at the other end, and little Vicki sat in the middle clutching Little Pillow, the worn-out old pillow she carried everywhere. Mrs. Zucker stood in front of them. "You know things have been a little hard for the family lately. . . ."

Caroline nodded. She knew exactly when the troubles had started. "I'm sorry the poor car died."

"Me, too," Patricia said.

"But it was funny," Vicki added. "I liked it when the light turned green and we couldn't go and all the people honked their horns."

Mrs. Zucker sighed. "It really wasn't funny, Vicki," she said. "I was awfully embarrassed."

"Your face turned all red," Patricia said.

Caroline remembered her mother trying to make the car start. They had to wait for the truck to come and tow them away. She didn't think it was funny, either.

Mrs. Zucker began to pace back and forth. "Your father and I hadn't planned to buy another car until next year, so I'm working extra hours at the hospital to help pay for it—not to mention trying to save enough money to get the dishwasher fixed."

Caroline knew how hard her mother was working. She was a nurse, and it seemed like she was never home anymore. Last night only their father had been there to kiss the girls good night. And the day before, their mother had slept through dinner because she was so tired.

"And now, Caroline and Vicki have birthdays coming," Mrs. Zucker went on.

At last, Caroline thought. Remembering Maria's ideas, she said, "I'd like a makeover party!"

Mrs. Zucker stopped pacing and stared down at her white nurse's shoes. "Honey, with all our money problems and all the time I'm spending at the hospital, it's going to be difficult having parties right now."

Caroline's mouth fell open. Parents couldn't cancel Christmas or the Fourth of July. How could they cancel a birthday? Vicki's eyes filled with tears. "No party?" they said together. Baxter whined in sympathy.

Mrs. Zucker raised her hands. "I didn't say there wouldn't be a party. But we're going to do things a little differently this year."

Vicki snuggled close to Caroline and whispered, "I *love* birthday parties!"

"Me, too." Caroline put her arm around her little sister and hugged her.

At the other end of the couch, Patricia frowned like someone who wished her birthday was coming soon, too.

13

"Since your birthdays are just fifteen days apart," Mrs. Zucker said to Caroline and Vicki, "your father and I have decided to have one big party for both of you."

Caroline couldn't believe her ears. *One party?* A party with Vicki and all her six-year-old friends? She scrunched her eyes shut, hoping that maybe she was dreaming.

But when she opened them again, she knew it wasn't a bad dream. There was going to be just one party for both her and Vicki, and she was sure her mother wouldn't listen to any arguments.

Caroline decided she had to try anyway. She had to tell her mother how she really felt. "My friends are going to *hate* coming to a party with Vicki and her friends," she cried.

Vicki pulled herself away from Caroline's arm and punched her. "What's wrong with my friends?"

"They're going to want to play baby games! And I'll bet half of them will wear Snuggle Kittens outfits!" Caroline cried, naming the TV cartoon characters that Vicki and her friends loved. She covered her face with her hands. "Everyone at school is going to laugh when they hear about my stupid party with the kindergarteners!"

"I don't want *your* friends at *my* party, either!" Vicki stuck out her lower lip in a pout.

Caroline folded her arms across her chest. "What's wrong with *my* friends?"

Vicki sat up as tall as she could. "They'll show off and act like they're more important because they're bigger than us. And they'll call us babies and laugh."

"Your friends wouldn't do that, Caroline, would they?" Mrs. Zucker asked as she sat on the arm of the couch.

Caroline drew a tic-tac-toe board on her jeans with her fingernail. Of course her friends would laugh. Hadn't she just said so?

Finally, she looked up at her mother. "My friends aren't going to like having a party with little kids."

"Stop complaining," Patricia said. "How do you think I feel? *Everyone* is going to have a party except me!"

"That's because it's not your birthday!" Caroline snapped. It wasn't her fault Patricia had been born in a different month.

"You'll have a party when the time comes," Mrs. Zucker told her.

15

"Yeah. And you won't have to share it with anyone, either," Caroline grumbled.

Her mother patted Caroline's shoulder. "I'm sorry you and Vicki don't like the idea. But it's the only way we can do it this year."

Caroline bit her lower lip. Her nose was itchy and there were hot tears behind her eyes, but she refused to be a crybaby.

"We need to start making plans right away." Mrs. Zucker smiled at Caroline and Vicki. "Do you have any party ideas? Do you know who you want to invite?"

Vicki scooted to the edge of the couch and grinned at her mother. "I want a clown!"

Caroline groaned. She could just hear her friends laughing themselves sick when some guy in a clown suit started acting goofy. Maria wouldn't laugh because she was Caroline's very best friend, but the others would.

Ignoring her sister, Vicki began her guest list. "I want to invite Mandy and Laura and Bonnie and . . ."

Caroline covered her ears. How could Vicki sound so happy about this party? It was going to be the biggest disaster that had ever happened in Homestead, Colorado!

3

IT'S TIME FOR HARRY'S GRILL

"I hate science," Caroline told Maria Wednesday afternoon.

"Since when?" Maria stretched across Caroline's bed and grabbed a smiling teddy bear by one leg. She tossed it at her friend. "You liked it when you got all the answers right on the test last week."

Caroline caught the bear and smoothed its fur. "Well, that was *last* week. I don't like it *this* week."

Caroline didn't like anything much since her mother had announced the two-in-one birthday party. It was absolutely the worst thing

18

that had ever happened to her in almost nine years. She wished Vicki had been born at some other time of year. And once, just for a second, she had wished Vicki hadn't been born at all.

"But our project is due next Thursday," Maria reminded her. "We have to start on it."

Caroline sighed. She set the bear on her desk and sat backwards in her chair, resting her chin on the back of it. "So what do you want to do?"

"It has to be something about sound. And I had an idea." Maria pulled a notebook and pencil out of her book bag. Flipping to a blank page, she drew a square. Then she drew a circle in the center of it. Caroline got out of her chair and came closer for a better look. She watched Maria draw five lines across the circle.

"What is it?" she asked.

Maria pointed to the circle in the center of the square. "Imagine this is a hole."

Caroline did. She looked at it a long time. Then she said, "It *could* be a guitar without a handle. . . ."

"Right!" Maria clapped her hands. Pointing to the five lines she had drawn, she explained, "These are rubber bands. We get different sized bands and stretch some tighter than others, and they'll each make a different sound when we *ping* them."

Caroline crooked her finger and pretended to pluck a guitar string. "You mean like this?"

"Exactly. Do you think we could learn to play a song on it?"

"Sure!" Caroline was impressed. She could see them standing in front of their class, amazing everybody with their instrument. "Let's play a song from the new Lucy Hanson tape."

Maria frowned. "We can try, but I'm not sure a rubber band guitar can do anything that hard."

Caroline wasn't worried. It was a great science project, much better than Samantha Collins's musical water glasses. She couldn't wait to get started.

"I'll find a box," she told Maria.

"I've got one at home," Maria said. "I thought we could paint it to look like wood."

"*You* could." Caroline wished she was as good at art as her friend. "But I'll come over to help."

Maria said seriously, "I can do most of the work if you want me to. You've got enough problems with your birthday party."

"Don't remind me!" Caroline groaned. She

pulled her pillow from beneath the blue-flowered quilt and buried her head under it.

"What are you going to do?" Maria asked.

"It's going to be a disaster. What *can* I do?" Caroline's brain overflowed with pictures of Vicki and all her little friends being so cute that it made her feel sick. "I just know Vicki is going to ruin everything."

"She's been pretty good lately," Maria said, trying to cheer Caroline up.

Caroline's laugh was muffled by the pillow. "Yeah. But just a year ago she was such a spoiled brat—always begging for attention. What if she turns bratty again in front of all our friends?"

"I bet she won't," Maria said. "Vicki's almost six. Acting like a baby would embarrass her, too. She'll behave."

"That'll be even worse!" Caroline took the pillow off her head. "Whenever she looks at anyone with those big eyes, they make a fuss over her and tell her how adorable she is. No one will remember it's *my* party, too. You're lucky you're an only child. You don't have to share everything."

Maria sighed. "Make up your mind. Are you worried that Vicki will act like a baby, or that everyone will pay more attention to her than you?"

Caroline shrugged her shoulders. "What does it matter? My party's wrecked either way."

"So what are you going to do about it?" Maria folded her hands in her lap, waiting for Caroline to come up with some ideas. Caroline was very good at making plans.

"There has to be a way I can convince my parents I need my own party," she told her friend.

"Of course there is," Maria said. "You always think of something."

That was exactly what Caroline had been telling herself. She always thought of something. Not long ago, she had figured out a way to convince her mother that she needed some pretty clothes like the other third-grade girls. At first, it had seemed like an impossible project, but now Caroline's closet was full of dresses, skirts and blouses. Her plan had finally worked.

"I think I'll try being *very* nice to my mom and dad," Caroline said after she thought about it for a while.

"How? Are you going to clean the house and stuff like that?"

Caroline frowned. "I didn't plan to work *that* hard. Maybe I could make dinner one night to surprise them."

"Or maybe do the ironing?" Maria suggested.

"Oh, no." Caroline shook her head. "The last time I tried to iron, I burned a hole in one of Dad's shirts. I guess the iron got too hot."

Maria made a check-mark in the air with one finger. "Forget ironing."

"Breakfast in bed might work. . . ." Caroline said, thinking out loud.

"That's a good idea," Maria said. "I bet they'd like it so much that they'd decide you deserve your very own party. But you have to work fast. Isn't the party supposed to be a week from Saturday?"

Caroline glanced at the calendar on the wall, the one with a new puppy picture for each month. Next Saturday's square was circled in black. "Yeah, that's when it is, all right. I can't waste any time."

"That's why *I'm* going to make our science project," Maria told her.

Caroline grinned. "Thanks!"

23

"What are friends for?" Maria asked just before Caroline almost strangled her with a hug.

"Thanks for dinner, Mrs. Zucker," Maria told Caroline's mother later that evening. "You make the best spaghetti." She headed for the family room.

When Caroline followed her, Patricia called, "Hey, Caroline, aren't you forgetting something?"

"*Please* wash the dishes for me tonight," Caroline begged her. "Maria and I *have* to watch *Harry's Grill.*" It was Caroline's favorite TV show. She couldn't miss it because of some dirty dishes!

With a sigh, Patricia asked, "What will I get for it?"

"I'll wash *and* dry tomorrow night," Caroline promised.

"Not enough. You have to scrub the bathtub, too."

Caroline scowled at her sister. "That's *your* job this week."

"Not if you want to see *Harry's Grill,*" Patricia teased.

In the family room, the theme song for the hit TV show began. As Caroline hurried out of the kitchen, she called over her shoulder, "Okay, it's a deal."

The show started with Harry telling someone in the next room that he wanted to create a new burger in honor of the town's eightieth anniversary. When Rich Strout, the teen-ager who played Thomas, came through the door, drying his wet blond hair with a towel, all the girls in the studio audience squealed and shouted. No one heard Harry's next line.

"He's so cute!" Maria whispered.

"Yeah," Caroline sighed. "Even cuter than Michael Hopkins."

Maria turned to stare at her. "Don't you still think Michael's the cutest boy in the whole third grade?"

After she checked that her sisters weren't listening, Caroline whispered, "Yes, but he doesn't smile like Thomas—I mean Rich Strout."

"Michael's only nine," Maria pointed out. "Give him time. Rich Strout must be *at least* sixteen years old."

They watched the show in silence until the first commercial. Then Caroline had to agree with Maria. "I guess it isn't really fair to compare Michael to him."

25

"And don't forget, Michael lives right here in Homestead," Maria said. "I bet Rich Strout lives in a big mansion in Hollywood. We'll never meet anyone like him."

"Shh . . . he's back." Caroline tucked her feet under her and leaned forward. It didn't matter that Rich Strout lived hundreds of miles away—she didn't want to miss one word he said, or one wonderful smile.

4

SAMANTHA'S AMAZING FAMILY

"I'm not sure I'll live," Caroline moaned as she and Maria staggered, shivering, into the classroom the next morning. Their teacher, Mrs. Nicks, hadn't arrived yet.

Maria gently touched her earlobes. "I know what you mean. Do I have frostbite? Have my ears turned white?"

Her friend's ears were pink, just like always. It really wasn't *that* cold outside. Caroline told her, "Your ears will survive."

"Thank goodness!" Maria heaved a huge sigh of relief. "I was afraid they'd fall off and then I wouldn't have anyplace to put my earrings!"

"What are you guys trying to do—act?" Samantha Collins said as she came over to them, brushing her long blond hair over her shoulders.

Caroline shoved her bangs out of her eyes. "Maybe." She knew her bangs were too long, but she didn't want to mention it to her mother. What if she took Caroline to the House of Beauty and told the woman to trim off a few inches all over? Then she'd never get a chance to grow her hair as long as Samantha's.

Samantha stuck her nose in the air. "Well, I know something about acting, and you guys are pretty bad."

"What do you know?" Maria asked. Mrs. Santiago designed costumes for the local theater, and Maria wanted to be an actress when she grew up. She knew a lot about being dramatic.

"I'm related to a famous actor," Samantha told them. She sounded so sure of herself that Caroline almost believed her.

Maria didn't. "Since when?" she demanded.

"Since last night," was Samantha's quick answer.

"Huh?" Caroline turned to Maria and saw that her friend was just as confused as she was.

Samantha smiled. It was obvious she was

28

dying to share some news. Everyone in Mrs. Nicks's class knew when Samantha had something important to say—she always shifted from foot to foot and her cheeks turned bright pink.

"Spit it out, Collins," Duncan Fairbush called from behind the girls. "We've got better things to do than wait all day for you to tell us about your *famous* relative."

"I bet it's Kermuggle!" one boy shouted, naming the little pig that was best friends with the Snuggle Kittens on their TV cartoon show.

Duncan snorted. "That pig can really act. *Oink!*"

"Real funny!" Samantha stamped her foot. "My Uncle Stanley got married yesterday—"

Duncan interrupted her to ask, "To Kermuggle?"

"Knock it off!" Caroline told him. "Let her finish."

Samantha didn't thank Caroline. She just continued, "He married Hannah Strout—Rich Strout's mother."

"Rich Strout!"

"Thomas on *Harry's Grill!*"

The news buzzed from girl to girl, but they all wondered whether or not to believe Samantha. At last Maria found her voice. *"Rich Strout* is your new *step-cousin?"*

Samantha's proud grin announced it was true. But she told them about it, anyway. "Yes! I'm Rich Strout's cousin!"

"Right," Duncan mumbled. "And my dad is the President of the United States!"

"Don't be so dumb," Caroline said to Duncan's back as the boys gathered by the window. Then she turned to Samantha. "Is he coming to visit you?"

How could she and Maria get to be better friends with Samantha? If Rich Strout ever came to visit the Collinses, they would just *have* to go over and look at him. Caroline wondered if Maria would agree to let Samantha join their private club. She'd ask her later if the Double Club could turn into the Triple Club.

Samantha shrugged and smiled smugly. "I don't know. My Uncle Stanley lives in California."

"Maybe they'll come to Colorado to go skiing," Maria suggested. It was obvious she wanted to meet Rich Strout as much as Caroline did.

"Maybe," Samantha said.

Mrs. Nicks came into the room and the

crowd scattered. On the way to their desks, Caroline whispered to Maria, "You can forget about inviting her to join Double Club."

"What?" Maria looked puzzled.

Caroline realized she hadn't told Maria about her plan to let Samantha join. There was no reason to tell her now. "Rich Strout is probably never going to visit Samantha," she said.

Maria sighed. "You're probably right. Why would any big Hollywood star want to visit a little town like Homestead?"

Caroline couldn't think of a single reason why Rich Strout would give up surfing in the ocean and hanging out with rock stars just to visit his new cousin. Life in California was too exciting.

Two hours later, Caroline bit her bottom lip as she tackled her math problems. Mrs. Nicks called it a re-naming assignment. But Caroline liked to think she was borrowing numbers from each other when she did subtraction problems.

She was trying to subtract eight from forty-five, but it was impossible to take the eight away from the five. "Knock, knock," she whispered to herself. She imagined the four in the tens column asking, "What do you want?" And she replied, "Ten ones, please."

Duncan Fairbush glanced over his shoulder and gave her a dirty look. Caroline smiled. Poor Duncan didn't know how to have fun with math.

While the class worked, Mrs. Nicks changed the display on the bulletin board. She took the old birthday notes down. Last month, she had written each person's name and birth date inside a musical note. Caroline wondered what her teacher would use this time.

Kevin's name went up first. His name was inside a yellow sun. His birthday was on Sunday, in just a few days. Caroline watched as her own sun was stapled next to Kevin's. She wished she could feel happy and proud, but she didn't.

The yellow construction paper sun looked so cheerful. It made her think of presents and parties. But she was going to have to share a party with Vicki—unless her plan worked. Under her desk, she crossed her fingers and hoped her parents would really appreciate it when she cooked dinner for the whole family the next night.

"Lunch time," Mrs. Nicks called from the front of the room. "Let's line up."

Caroline went over to Maria's desk. Her friend pointed to the bulletin board. "I like your sun."

"I feel like it's staring at me. It's daring me to fix things before the disaster party," Caroline whispered. She didn't want the whole class to hear her.

"You can do it," Maria whispered back as they joined the lunch line.

In front of them, some other girls were reading the birthday suns. Caroline tried hard not to listen to them, but she couldn't help herself.

"Caroline's birthday is next week," Betsy Boggs said.

Samantha pointed to Caroline's sun. "Next Thursday."

"Have you been invited to her party?" Betsy asked Samantha.

Instead of admitting that she hadn't been invited, Samantha asked, "Have you?" It didn't take them long to discover that no one had received an invitation to Caroline's party. Caroline hadn't been able to decide which would be worse—not inviting anyone at all, or having the girls from her class find out she had to share her party with a six-year-old.

"I can't stand it!" she told Maria. "If I have to share my party with Vicki, then I'm moving to Australia!"

5

FROZEN PEAS ARE CRUNCHY

"Thanks for calling, Mrs. White." Laurie Morrell hung up the phone, then tried to find a pencil in the Zuckers' kitchen. It was Friday evening. Laurie worked for Caroline's parents, baby-sitting the Zucker girls most afternoons. Mr. Zucker was her high-school history teacher.

She continued to search under the recipe cards Caroline had scattered over the counter. To keep from forgetting the message, she muttered, "Mandy White. Mandy White."

"What about Mandy White?" Caroline asked,

35

pulling a stubby pencil out of her jeans pocket and handing it to Laurie.

Laurie quickly wrote down the name on a note pad that Mrs. Zucker kept by the phone. "That was Mandy's mom. She called to say Mandy will be coming to Vicki's birthday party—and yours."

"*Vicki's* party," Caroline corrected. "After Mom and Dad eat the wonderful dinner you're helping me cook, I'm sure they'll let me have a party of my very own."

Laurie sighed. "I don't know, Caroline. . . ."

"Don't you think a nine-year-old girl *deserves* her own party?" Caroline put on an apron and started stirring bread crumbs into the meatloaf.

"Well, yes, but it's not up to me," Laurie said.

"It doesn't matter," Caroline told Laurie. "After tonight, things will be fine."

Laurie added chopped onions to the meatloaf. As she mixed the ingredients, she said, "I hope you're not going to be disappointed."

"Don't worry," Caroline said as she dragged a bag of potatoes out of the cupboard under the counter. "It'll be okay."

Patricia came dashing into the kitchen and

skidded to a stop. She looked around. "What a mess! Mom's going to have a fit!"

Caroline glanced at the clock over the stove. "She won't be home for an hour, and Dad will probably be even later. We'll have everything under control by then."

Patricia backed out of the room. "Well, just don't ask me to help when Mom or Dad walks in the door and everything's still a mess."

"I wouldn't ask you to help if the *world* was ending!" Caroline shouted. She didn't want anyone else to share the credit for dinner.

Laurie opened the oven door and put the meatloaf pan on the top rack. Then she set the timer. "Now Caroline, the meatloaf needs to bake for an hour," Laurie said. "The buzzer will sound when it's ready."

"No problem." Caroline dropped seven potatoes into the sink and began to scrub them.

"It's not as easy as it seems," Laurie warned. "You have to make sure everything gets done at the same time—the meatloaf, the potatoes, and the peas. And don't forget about the cake. Plus, you'll have to clean up the kitchen and set the table. Your mother knows I have to leave a little early tonight for my date, so you're on your own for now."

37

Caroline didn't see why Laurie was making such a fuss. She was sure she could handle everything just fine. After all, she was almost nine.

Nearly an hour later, the potato peels had gone down the disposal and all the bowls and knives had been rinsed in the sink. Caroline stirred water into the packaged cake mix, put it in the microwave, and set the timer. The potatoes and the frozen peas were in saucepans on the stove, but the table wasn't set yet.

Caroline grabbed some silverware and set five places. She had planned to fold the napkins in some fancy way, but there wasn't enough time.

"I'm hungry," Vicki whined, trotting into the kitchen with Little Pillow trailing behind her. "Can I have a bowl of cereal?"

Caroline couldn't believe that her sister wanted to eat cereal when a wonderful dinner was almost ready. "You can wait and eat with the rest of us," she said.

"But *you're* cooking it." Vicki stared at Caroline with big, innocent brown eyes.

"So?"

Vicki continued to stare at Caroline without blinking. "So I hope we can eat it."

Under her breath, Caroline counted to ten. She told herself not to be mad at Vicki. What did her baby sister know about cooking dinner?

They both heard a car in the driveway. Vicki ran to tell Patricia that one of their parents had come home. Caroline quickly poured two small glasses of cranberry juice.

"Something smells good," Mr. Zucker announced, coming through the back door. "Is your mother home already, sweetie?"

Caroline gave him a kiss and smiled proudly. "*I'm* cooking dinner tonight!"

He ruffled her hair. "Good for you!"

"Want a drink before supper?" Caroline handed her father a glass of juice.

Mr. Zucker set his briefcase on the counter. "What a nice idea. I could get used to being spoiled this way," he said as he drank his juice.

Caroline was very happy. If her mother was only half as impressed, she could start planning her big-kids-only party before bedtime!

As her father went out of the kitchen, the oven timer buzzed. Caroline took out the meatloaf. Then she hurried to drain the potatoes. But the peas still weren't boiling. Puzzled, she lifted the pan and looked at the electric burner. It was black and cold, but the one behind it was red hot. She had turned on the wrong one! Quickly, Caroline moved the pan to the hot burner.

She planned to mash the potatoes next, but then the microwave timer sounded. Was her cake really done already? Caroline decided to bake it ten minutes longer, just to make sure.

"What's going on here?" Mrs. Zucker asked. Caroline had been so busy that she hadn't heard her come in.

"Dinner," Caroline told her. "I'm cooking dinner." She gave the second glass of juice to her mother. Then she hurried back to the potatoes. She didn't have time to talk.

Ten minutes later, everyone sat down at the table. Caroline couldn't stop grinning as she brought over the mashed potatoes, buttered peas and meatloaf.

"This looks wonderful," Mr. Zucker said.

"Smells good, too," Mrs. Zucker said, smiling.

Vicki held out her plate for the first slice of meatloaf. Patricia helped herself to some potatoes, and Mrs. Zucker served the peas. Caroline was very proud of herself. Everything

40

looked just the way it should. She was almost too excited to eat.

"These peas are hard!" Vicki cried, making a face.

Caroline stabbed a few with her fork and put them into her mouth. Vicki was right—they crunched between her teeth. And they were still cold in the middle.

"It's not my fault that the water wouldn't boil," Caroline mumbled.

"There are *lumps* in the potatoes! They're as big as rocks," Patricia said.

"Lumps? What lumps?" Mr. Zucker asked, pretending he hadn't noticed.

"The meatloaf is delicious," Mrs. Zucker said. "You did a good job, Caroline."

But all Caroline had done to the meatloaf was to add the bread crumbs. Laurie had done the rest.

"Do I have to eat my hard peas?" Vicki asked.

"No, sweetheart," her mother told her.

Patricia didn't even ask if she had to eat her food. She just pushed her plate away.

Caroline didn't feel proud anymore. She felt embarrassed. And then she remembered the cake. "Wait!" she cried. "I made dessert!"

"Yay!" Vicki cried.

Caroline had left the cake inside the microwave to keep it hidden. Now she smiled to herself when she lifted it out. Dinner had been a disaster, but she was sure the dessert would be a success.

"You can cut it," she told her mother. She handed her a knife and put the cake in front of her.

Mrs. Zucker set the knife blade on top of the cake and pressed down on it. The knife wouldn't budge. Then she tried to saw it back and forth. Nothing happened. Turning to Caroline, she asked, "Is this a trick cake, honey?"

Patricia reached over and tapped the cake with her spoon. It made a thumping sound. "It's hard as wood," she said.

Mrs. Zucker poked it with her finger. "It feels like plastic. How long did you leave it in the microwave, Caroline?"

Before Caroline could answer, Vicki moaned, "I'm hungry!" Caroline's stomach grumbled in agreement.

"Do we have to eat just meatloaf?" Patricia asked, wrinkling her nose.

Mr. Zucker glanced at Caroline, who was trying very hard not to cry. He cleared his throat and looked across the table at her mother.

42

"You know, Marsha, this meatloaf would make great sandwiches for our lunch tomorrow."

Mrs. Zucker nodded. "You're right, dear. We can both take big, fat sandwiches to work."

"But what will we eat tonight?" Caroline asked sadly.

Patricia started to pound on the table. "Piz-za! Piz-za!"

Vicki picked up the rhythm and joined her. "Piz-za! Piz-za!"

"I know how hard you tried to make a nice dinner, honey," Mrs. Zucker told Caroline gently, "but pizza sounds awfully good to me right now."

Caroline had to admit that she would rather have pizza, too. But she still had to solve her problem. Crunchy peas, lumpy potatoes and wooden cake were not going to convince her parents to give her a separate birthday party. Caroline would have to come up with another plan, and fast!

6

LAST CHANCE

"Be quiet!" Caroline mumbled to her clock radio the next morning. She buried her head under her pillow, but the radio continued to blare. The disc jockey sounded very cheerful as he cried, "Good morning, early birds! What are your plans for this beautiful Saturday morning in Colorado?"

Caroline sat up in bed and rubbed her eyes. She had very important plans for this morning. She had to put on some clothes and find her dad before he went jogging without her. Running along beside him, there would be no one to interrupt her while she told him how

45

important it was for her to have her own birthday party.

She crossed her fingers, but it was impossible to pull up her blue sweat pants that way. Caroline peered at the fishbowl in the corner. Neither Justin nor Esmerelda looked very wide awake.

"Sorry if I'm bothering you guys," she told them with a yawn. "But I have to hurry. I just know Dad's going to listen to me. And then he'll let me have my own party. I know he will."

She tucked her allowance in the back pocket of her sweat pants. After saying good-bye to the goldfish, she galloped down the steps from her attic bedroom. Her father was just opening the front door. "Wait for me!" Caroline called.

"Shh . . ." Mr. Zucker put a finger to his lips. "Everyone else is sleeping. Why are you up so early?"

"To go jogging with you." She pointed to her running shoes.

"You haven't run with me for a while," he said. "What's the occasion?"

"I need some fresh air." Caroline didn't want to tell him what was on her mind just yet.

Her father stepped outside and sucked in a

deep breath. "There's a lot of fresh air out here."

The sun was peeking over the mountains as they started to run. Caroline loved jogging with her father. He always ran more slowly than usual so she could keep up with him—or just behind him.

"Hey, Dad . . ." Caroline's words seemed to drift away behind her, so she ran harder to catch up with her father.

He smiled down at her. "It's fun having a running partner."

"It's fun being alone with you," she told him.

"We don't get much time alone, do we?"

It might have been a good time for her to mention the party, but Caroline decided to lead up to it gradually.

"How's school?" Mr. Zucker asked.

Caroline told him about the science project she was doing with Maria, and that Rich Strout was Samantha Collins's new cousin.

"You haven't mentioned Duncan," her father observed as they jogged along. "Is he still in your class?"

"Yes. And he's as horrible as ever." Caroline bit her lower lip. There was a pain in her side.

She was afraid she wouldn't be able to keep up with her father much longer.

"Getting tired?" he asked when she fell behind him.

"Just a little," Caroline panted. "But I could run as far as the Quick Mart."

He laughed. "And what would we do at the Quick Mart?"

"Have juice and a doughnut?"

"Good idea." He patted the pocket of his running shorts. "But I didn't bring any money."

Caroline grinned. "I did."

The Quick Mart had three little booths in the back. They sat across from each other, sipping their juice.

"Caroline . . ." Her father set down his bottle. "Did you come with me today because you want to talk about something?" He was so smart. Caroline figured that was why he was a high-school teacher. Laurie said he knew *everything* about history.

"I'm going to be nine next week," she began.

"Nine?" He sighed. "It seems like you were a baby only last year or the year before. . . ."

"I haven't been a baby for *nine years,*" she told him.

48

"You're right." He bit into his glazed dough-nut.

"But Vicki's still kind of a baby," Caroline pointed out.

Mr. Zucker put down his doughnut. "Does this have anything to do with the party?"

"Vicki is only turning six. I'm going to be nine on Thursday. There's a big difference," Caroline said.

"And?"

"And that's why it would be awful for us to share a birthday party! My friends are going to laugh themselves to death when they see Vicki and her baby friends."

Her father shook his head. "I wish I could help you, honey."

"You *can* help me," she told him. "Talk to Mom."

"Hmm." He folded his hands on the table. "The joint party isn't just your mom's idea, you know, Caroline. I agree with her."

Caroline swallowed hard. "How *can* you? It's a *terrible* idea!"

Mr. Zucker explained. "I'm sorry, but we're short on money right now. The party is going to be great. Give it a chance, okay?"

Give it a chance? Caroline thought. That was

easy for him to say. When the party was a bomb, it wasn't *his* friends who would tease him about it for weeks and weeks. What was she going to do?

When Caroline and her father got home, breakfast was waiting for them. Mrs. Zucker didn't have to work that morning, so she'd made pancakes.

"Yum!" Caroline cried. Then she gave a worried glance at her father. Would her mother get mad if she knew they'd already eaten some doughnuts before breakfast? Mothers could get real funny about things like that. But Mr. Zucker just gave Caroline a quick wink and smiled—their pre-breakfast treat was their own little secret.

Caroline smiled back at him as she sat down at the table. Sharing a secret with her father made her feel grown-up. Besides, she knew she'd have no problem finishing her pancakes. They were her favorite!

"Remember when I tried to run with you?" Patricia asked Mr. Zucker.

"As I recall, we got almost to the corner before you begged to come back home," her father said with a smile.

Patricia made a face. "I'd rather practice the piano ten hours a day than go jogging." Then she added quickly, "It's not that I don't like being with you, Dad, but I'm not very good at running, and I'm *very* good at playing the piano."

Caroline sighed. Of course her sister liked playing the piano. Patricia's teacher kept telling her how talented she was, and Patricia kept telling everybody else the same thing.

Mr. Zucker smiled at Caroline. "We had a good time this morning, didn't we, honey?"

Caroline wanted to say, "We had a good time until you said I couldn't have my own party." But she didn't.

Then Mrs. Zucker started collecting the breakfast dishes, and Caroline jumped out of her chair to help her. Mr. Zucker went out of the kitchen to change his clothes.

"Sit down for a minute, honey," her mother told her. "The dishes can wait for a while. I want to talk to you and Vicki."

She took a notebook from the counter and sat down at the table again. Caroline didn't have to guess what she wanted to talk about. It had to be the party.

"Can I stay, too?" Patricia asked.

"Sure." Mrs. Zucker tapped her pen on the open notebook. "I've hired a clown for you, Vicki."

Caroline's youngest sister clapped her hands. "Ooh, good!"

"He's not a professional clown," Mrs. Zucker admitted. "His mother works with me in the hospital. But we can afford him."

Caroline groaned. It wasn't bad enough that they were having a clown—he would probably be a *bad* clown!

"We don't have much time left. The party is a week from today," Mrs. Zucker went on. "I have Vicki's guest list and I've found her a clown. Now, what do you want, Caroline?"

Holding her head high, Caroline said, "I want my own party."

"Besides that."

"All I want is my own party," she repeated.

Mrs. Zucker closed her notebook with a snap and stood up. "I give up, Caroline! You have had every chance to help plan this party. If you don't care, then I can't do anything for you at all." She turned her back on the girls abruptly, and brought the dishes over to the sink.

Caroline's mouth fell open. She knew her mother was tired from working so hard and from worrying about money. But her mother had never given up on her before—not even when she'd locked everyone out of the house on the coldest day of the year when she was five years old.

Patricia patted her hand. "Want to draw pictures with me? You can use my new markers."

Caroline almost said no. After all, coloring was a kid thing. But she didn't have anything better to do—nothing fun, like planning her very own party. Her sister was just trying to help.

"Sure," she sighed. "Let's go to your room."

7

SURPRISE!

"Are we going to have a Double Club meeting?" Caroline asked Maria on Tuesday afternoon. She had walked home with Maria after school. The Santiagos' house looked the same as usual, but Caroline had a funny feeling that something was different.

Maria hung her hot pink jacket on the coat rack in the entryway. When she turned to Caroline, her dark eyes were sparkling. "No. It's not a club meeting."

"It's the science project, right? You need help with our guitar?"

"Not quite. Come up to my room."

Maria was acting very mysterious. Caroline followed her friend upstairs and down the hall to her bedroom. What she saw through the doorway took her breath away. The room was filled with brightly colored balloons! Graceful pink and white streamers hung from the skylight in the ceiling.

"What's going on?" Caroline gasped.

From nowhere, Mrs. Santiago appeared with a little cake. There were nine candles burning on top of it. She set it on Maria's desk. Then the two of them began singing, "Happy birthday to you . . ."

Caroline felt a happy tear slide down her cheek. "For *me?* This is for *me?*"

"Don't try to put out the candles with tears," Mrs. Santiago joked. "You have to blow them out."

"All of them!" Maria added.

Caroline took a deep breath and blew. Every single candle went out.

Maria's mother stayed long enough to cut the cake and pour some punch. Then she went back downstairs.

"This is amazing!" Caroline told her friend.

Maria bit into a piece of cake and tried to catch the crumbs that fell past her chin. "And do you know the best part? No six-year-olds are allowed at this party!"

Caroline ate three pieces of the cake and Maria ate two. Then she gave Caroline her present.

"But it's not my birthday for two days," Caroline said, staring at the brightly wrapped gift. "Maybe you should save it for my party on Saturday."

"No. Open it now," Maria said.

Then Caroline had a horrible thought. "Aren't you coming on Saturday? Is that why you're doing this today?"

Maria grinned. "I'll be there. I might even have another present for you."

Caroline couldn't wait any longer. She ripped the paper off the little package. "Lucy Hanson's new tape! I love you, Maria Santiago!"

They threw their arms around each other in a giant hug. Maria looked shy when she said, "I thought you would like it."

"Can we play it?" Caroline took Maria's Lucy Hanson tape out of the cassette player and put her own into the slot.

"It's the same tape," Maria told her.

Caroline held her breath until the first song began. "But *this* tape is mine!"

Leaving the cake crumbs and punch cups on the desk, they both stretched out on Maria's bed. While Lucy Hanson sang in the background, Caroline said softly, "I'm almost nine."

"It's kinda weird, being nine," Maria said.

"Why?"

Maria tapped her chin with a finger while she thought. Then she rolled on her back and looked up at the streamers. "Well, I'm not a little kid anymore. But I'm still not old enough to do really neat stuff like wear makeup."

"Think your mom will let you do that when you're ten?" Caroline asked.

Maria shook her head. "Not until middle school."

"Same with my mom," Caroline told her. "Do you think they get together and decide things?"

"No." Maria touched one sparkly earring. "Because I have pierced ears and you don't."

Caroline sighed. "I wish I could get mine pierced, but Mom says I have to wait until sixth grade."

She thought some more about what it would

be like being nine. "Do you think Michael Hopkins will like me?"

Maria's hand flew to her heart in one of her dramatic gestures. "*What?* Have you forgotten Rich Strout already?"

"We'll never meet him," Caroline told her. "Do you really believe he's Samantha's cousin?"

Maria batted a red balloon at Caroline. "Why would she lie about something like that?"

Caroline sat up and punched a blue balloon at Maria's head. "I just bet she would, that's all."

Soon Samantha was forgotten when the girls started a giggling balloon fight.

"Girls, what on earth are you doing?" Mrs. Santiago asked from the doorway.

"Being nine!" Maria yelled.

"So that's what it means to be nine these days," her mother said, as if she'd discovered something amazing. "Funny—you used to like doing things like this when you were four." She smiled at both girls. "I hate to break up the party, but it's time for me to drive Caroline home."

Caroline didn't want to go. There was still some cake and punch left. And it had been so much fun talking about getting older, without any little sisters around to interrupt.

"Can't I just live here for a few days?" she asked Mrs. Santiago. "Like until Saturday night?"

"You'd miss your party," Maria's mother answered.

"That's the whole idea," Maria said.

Caroline said sadly, *"This* party is the best thing that's going to happen for my birthday. I just know it. I don't even want to go to my *other* party on Saturday."

Maria hugged Caroline again. "I'll be there," she said. "We'll make it okay, you'll see."

Caroline smiled at Maria. "Thanks for the surprise, and the tape."

"The tape!" Maria cried. She took the cassette out of the player and slipped it back into its case. "This Lucy is yours. Don't forget her!"

"I won't," Caroline said. She pressed the Lucy Hanson tape to her cheek. No matter what happened on Saturday, she knew she was very lucky to have a best friend like Maria.

8

HAPPY BIRTHDAY, CAROLINE!

On Thursday morning, Caroline hopped out of bed and rushed to her dresser mirror. She leaned close and stared at her face. Turning to her right, she studied one side. Then she turned her left side to the mirror. Finally, she backed up to the dresser and peered over one shoulder.

"I suppose you wonder what I'm doing," she said to her goldfish. "I'm trying to see if I changed during the night. I'm nine now!"

Justin and Esmerelda swam to the top of their bowl. Caroline wanted to believe they were listening to her, but she knew they were just hungry. She took a few seconds to feed them before she got dressed.

When she came downstairs, her father looked up from his bowl of cereal and whistled.

Caroline spun around to show off her clothes. She had saved one of her very favorite outfits to wear today. She thought her short plaid skirt made her look older. And she loved the way her blue tights matched one part of the plaid, while her bulky purple sweater repeated another color.

Patricia stopped eating to say, "I like your hair."

"Really?" Caroline smiled. A wide headband kept her hair from falling in her eyes. Now that it was getting longer, she had to worry about it getting in her way.

"Caroline, sit down." Her father waved his hand toward her chair. "I have to leave soon and I don't want to miss anything."

"Like what?" Caroline sat down, but no one handed her a cereal bowl.

Instead, Mrs. Zucker cleared the table while Patricia scooted into the family room. She returned with three packages.

"Are those for me?" Caroline asked, excited.

"If you don't want them, I'll take them," Patricia offered. But she placed the pile of presents in front of Caroline.

Vicki pointed to the lumpiest package. "Open mine first! I wrapped it myself."

Caroline felt something hard like a stick inside the Snuggle Kittens wrapping paper. Vicki was squirming in her chair with excitement as Caroline unwrapped her gift.

"This is great!" she cried. "Thanks, Vicki!"

It was a thick pen with three colors of ink. And not just red, blue and black like some kids had at school. This pen could write in pink, lavender, or light blue. Caroline flipped the wrapping paper upside down and wrote her name in each color on the back of it.

"There are other presents," her father reminded her.

The next package jingled. A piece of paper taped to it said: *To Caroline. From Patricia.*

When Caroline ripped open the package, a lot of bright-colored plastic animals fell onto the table. "What is this?" she asked.

Patricia couldn't wait for Caroline to take a closer look at her gift. "It's a belt!"

Caroline picked it up. The animals were at-

62

tached to a green plastic chain. Caroline had seen some first-graders wearing belts like it.

"I wanted one for myself, but I only had enough money to buy one," Patricia explained.

"Thanks, Patricia." Caroline felt a lump in her throat. Her sister had given her something very special, even if it wasn't what she would have chosen for herself. "You can borrow it sometimes."

Patricia smiled. "Thanks!"

Now Caroline unwrapped the biggest package. Under the paper she found a Bernard's box. Crossing her fingers, she hoped there were clothes inside. She had pointed out several outfits the last time she and her mother were in the department store.

"Read the card," Mrs. Zucker said.

Though Caroline was dying to find out what was inside the box, she took the card out of the envelope. She saw her very own face smiling at her. "It's me!"

"Do you like it?" Mrs. Zucker asked. "Mrs. Santiago drew it."

"I love it!"

Caroline opened the card. Inside, her mother had written: *Happy Ninth Birthday. Each year you get smarter and prettier. This year will be the best yet. Love, Mom and Dad.*

Caroline put down the card and opened the box. When she saw the black-and-white sweater, she cried, "I don't believe it!" She had been wanting the sweater for ages, but the last time she'd checked the sale rack in Bernard's girls' department, there weren't any left in her size. Her mom was sure sneaky.

"There's more," Mrs. Zucker told her with a smile.

Caroline took a pale green dress out of the box. The fabric was soft and fuzzy. She loved the way it felt when she held it against her cheek. "Thank you, Mom," she said. "These are really super clothes."

Patricia said, "I'm going to have super clothes when I'm in third grade, too."

At the end of the table, Mr. Zucker pretended to search his pockets. He acted startled when he found a small box. As he handed it to Caroline, he said, "This must be for you."

"Thank you, Dad." Caroline lifted the lid off the tiny box. She gasped when she saw what was inside. "It's a beautiful locket!"

"There might be something inside it," her father suggested.

64

Caroline snapped open the heart-shaped locket and found a photograph of a round-faced baby. "Is this me?" she asked.

He nodded. "When you were two days old."

"Let me see," Vicki cried. She and Patricia crowded close to look at the picture.

"I want to put a picture of you and Mom on the other side," Caroline told her father.

He smiled. "I was hoping you'd say that."

9

KIDNAPPED!

A few hours later, it was time for Caroline's class to present their science projects.

Samantha Collins brought her musical glasses to the front of the class. She had filled them with different amounts of water. Each glass played a note when she tapped it. To show off her wonderful project, she played "Yankee Doodle." Her partner just stood against the chalkboard with her hands in her pockets.

Caroline smiled to herself. At least she and Maria were going to play one of Lucy Hanson's songs together.

Mrs. Nicks clapped when Samantha finished her song. The rest of the class joined her. Then it was Duncan Fairbush's turn. He went to the front of the room and shouted through a paper towel tube. *Boring,* Caroline thought.

"Caroline and Maria?" The teacher glanced at them. "Would you like to go next?"

"Sure." Maria carried their guitar to the front of the room and Caroline followed her. She was sure Mrs. Nicks would like the way Maria and her mom had painted the cardboard box to make it look like real wood.

First, Caroline described how the instrument had been made. Then Maria explained why rubber bands stretched to different lengths made different sounds.

Duncan looked puzzled, but Caroline thought their explanation was very good. It wasn't their problem if Duncan didn't understand. What could you expect from someone who shouted through tubes?

"Now we're going to play the first verse of 'Happiness,'"Maria told the class. Several of the girls whispered to each other—they were Lucy Hanson fans, too.

Caroline and Maria had learned a two-part harmony. Maria whispered, "One, two, three . . ." to get the rhythm started, and they began to pluck the strings.

Suddenly a rubber band popped loose and snapped Caroline's fingers. *"Ow!"* she cried. She could hear Duncan snickering in the back of the room.

Maria glanced at the teacher. "Sorry—it never did this before."

She hooked it back in place, and they started again. They got through the first two lines of the song before one of Maria's bands broke and snapped both of their hands.

"I can't fix it," Maria wailed. "I didn't bring any extra rubber bands."

"It's all right," Mrs. Nicks told them. "We got a good idea of your project. It was very creative."

Duncan muttered, "It was dumb. And Zucker's part of it was the dumbest."

Maria planted her hands on her hips. "Don't you be mean to Caroline, Duncan Fairbush! Today's her birthday!"

"Oooh!" Duncan grinned. "A birthday! Big deal! Hey, everybody, let's sing 'Happy Birthday' to Zucker!" He started to sing, and some of the other kids in the class joined him:

"Happy Birthday to you,
You belong in the zoo!
You look like a monkey,
And you act like one, too!"

"Class! Class!" Mrs. Nicks shouted over the noise. "That is quite enough!"

Maria handed the broken instrument to the teacher and the girls went back to their desks. She whispered to Caroline, "I hope Duncan didn't ruin your birthday."

"I wouldn't let Duncan Fairbush ruin *anything,* especially not my birthday," Caroline whispered back. But then she thought about her two-for-one party. On Saturday she was going to be more embarrassed than the time she had gotten sick at Grandpa Nevelson's candy store. She had invited eight girls from her class to a party with giggling six-year-olds and an amateur clown. What could possibly be worse?

"Aren't we having dinner?" Patricia asked when everyone gathered in the Zuckers' living room around six o'clock that night.

"In a while," her mother said.

"But shouldn't someone be cooking it?" Caroline's stomach growled.

70

"Let your mom rest a few minutes, honey," her father said. "She worked hard today."

Caroline knew they couldn't possibly be waiting for *her* to cook dinner, not after last week's disaster. Suddenly she saw headlights in the driveway.

"Who's here?" Caroline asked, but nobody answered her. They all just stared at the front door as it opened. A tall man with a scarf tied over his face growled, "Everyone into the car!"

Caroline was scared. She glanced at her father, expecting him to do something to protect his family. But he simply reached for his jacket. Their mother did the same thing. What was going on?

Then Caroline looked closely at the man in the doorway. There was something very familiar about him. . . .

Finally, Vicki couldn't control herself any longer. She ran toward the man and threw herself into his arms. "You're so *funny,* Grandpa Nevelson!" she squealed.

Caroline couldn't believe he'd fooled her. Of course, he was wearing a plaid wool jacket she had never seen before. She'd never seen him with a scarf covering most of his face, either.

"Where are we going?" Caroline asked excitedly.

"Don't ask questions. Just get your jacket," he said in the same growly voice. Once Caroline was bundled up, he ordered, "Come here and turn around."

When she did, he untied his scarf and wrapped it around her eyes like a blindfold. "Now my plans will remain a surprise, unless your sisters can't keep a secret," he said.

"Take my hand," her father told Caroline as they went outside. He led her down the steps and into a car. Caroline was pretty sure it was Grandpa Nevelson's big old station wagon.

It seemed like the car bumped along the road forever until her grandfather called, "We're here! Take off the blindfold."

Hands fussed to untie the scarf knotted behind her head. When the unseen helper tugged too hard, Caroline cried, "Ouch! Don't pull my hair."

"Sorry," Patricia answered quickly.

Then the scarf fell away and Caroline saw where they were. "Mile-High Diner! My favorite restaurant in the whole world!" she cried.

The hostess led them to a table right away because Grandpa Nevelson had made reservations. Caroline couldn't stop smiling. She loved adventures and surprises!

"Sit across from me," Grandpa Nevelson instructed. "I want to look at my birthday girl."

"And I want to look at *you*," Caroline told him. "Thank you for the neat present."

"Present? You think this is your present?"

"Isn't it?" she asked.

His brown eyes sparkled. "What good is a dinner? You can't keep it under your pillow or take it to school to show your friends, can you?"

He was right. But Caroline didn't really expect anything more. Then Grandpa Nevelson set a big package on the table.

Caroline ripped off the striped wrapping paper and peeked under the lid of the box. What was inside? She lifted the brightly colored package. When she read the words on it, she gasped, "This is *too* neat!"

Vicki tried to climb into Mrs. Zucker's lap to get a good look. "What is it?" she asked.

Caroline grinned. "Crystals. It's a kit to grow crystals!" She turned the front of the box toward the others so they could see the pictures. "Red ones and blue ones and pointy white ones."

73

Grandpa Nevelson beamed at her. "I thought you might like to try some experiments."

"It's not going to make yucky smells, is it?" Patricia wrinkled her nose. "Janie Smith has a chemistry set, and it stinks!"

"This will just make pretty crystals." Caroline gazed across the table. "Thanks, Grandpa Nevelson. It's a wonderful present."

He smiled. "You are very welcome, Caroline. And now let's decide what we're going to eat. You can order anything you want, birthday girl."

As Caroline studied the menu, she knew she was a very lucky person. Adding up the party at Maria's house, and the presents at breakfast, and the Mile-High Diner, she had to admit her birthday had been fun. She just hoped the happy memories would make her smile during the horrible party on Saturday.

10

A DISASTER WAITING TO HAPPEN

"I can't do it," Caroline said to her stuffed animals and her goldfish on Saturday morning. She picked up the blue bunny that lived on her bed and told him, "I just can't face what's going on downstairs!"

When the rabbit didn't offer any sympathy, she turned to her stuffed bear. "Laurie's helping Mom and Patricia decorate for the party. They don't need my help. I'd only be in the way."

The bear wasn't any more sympathetic than the rabbit had been. Caroline peered into the fishbowl, but Justin and Esmerelda completely ignored her.

"I don't care what any of you think," she told them all. "I can't stand to see all those balloons and streamers and Snuggle Kitten cutouts. The living room's going to look like a kindergarten! This party is going to be the worst thing that ever happened in my entire life!"

She checked her watch and groaned. Twelve o'clock, and the party wasn't until one. But Caroline had already put on her new green dress. It had long sleeves, a rounded neck, and a dropped waistline. It was the most grown-up dress she had ever owned. She was wearing the heart-shaped locket, too. There were two pictures in it now—her baby picture, and one of her parents that she had cut out of a family photograph.

The locket was probably the best present she had ever received. Her dad knew she was growing up—he wouldn't have given the beautiful locket to a little kid. So why were her parents still making her share her ninth birthday with a bunch of kindergarten kids?

Maria was the first to arrive. Caroline met her at the door.

"You look terrific," Maria told her as she

came inside. "I love your new dress. And the party decorations are really neat."

Caroline mumbled, "I think I'm going to be sick."

Maria grabbed her by the shoulders. "Caroline Zucker, stop feeling sorry for yourself! The rest of the girls will be here any minute. You can't let them see that you're upset."

Caroline raised her chin. Maria was right. Maybe this wasn't the kind of party she wanted, but she didn't have to let everyone know how disappointed she was. And she couldn't spoil Vicki's fun, either. She'd pretend to enjoy herself if it killed her.

The doorbell rang. Caroline opened the door and found Mandy White waiting on the steps. She smiled at the little redheaded girl and let her in.

Soon the house was packed with big girls and little girls. Caroline's father had muttered something about work he just *had* to do at school, and sneaked out the back door. Mrs. Zucker and Laurie Morrell were in charge.

"Aren't they cute?" Maria asked Betsy Boggs, looking across the room at Vicki and her little friends.

"Cute?" Betsy made a face. "They remind me

of my little sister. She drew all over my stamp collection last week—with *permanent marker!*"

"Sisters aren't so bad," Caroline told her.

"Is that why you're sharing your party with these munchkins?" Priscilla Wilson asked.

"Let's forget about them," Maria said quickly. "Did you like the new dress Mrs. Nicks wore yesterday?"

"Yuck!" the girls cried in unison.

"She looks *awful* in black," Diane Buckley said.

Lisa Andrews put in, "At least it was something different. Have you ever noticed how many times she wears that red skirt with the big pockets?"

"Twice last week," Caroline answered.

Then Susan Ryan said, "What did you think of Samantha's Yankee Doodle glasses?"

Samantha hadn't arrived yet. It wasn't usual for her to be late, and Caroline wondered if maybe she wasn't coming at all.

Maria giggled. "I kept wishing that Duncan would sip some water from one of the glasses. Then it would have played the wrong note and she wouldn't have known why!"

"Maria Santiago!" Lisa was shocked. "That

sounds exactly like something Duncan would do. When did you start thinking like him?"

"Your guitar was neat," Wendy told Caroline and Maria.

Priscilla nodded. "I'd rather hear part of a Lucy Hanson song on rubber bands than *all* of 'Yankee Doodle.' "

Suddenly the honking of a horn interrupted them and Vicki's clown burst into the living room. He had a curly wig, and a huge red nose, and he was wearing a checkered suit and enormous yellow shoes. When Vicki pinched his nose, it honked, and all the little girls squealed with delight.

"Want to go upstairs and listen to my new Lucy tape?" Caroline asked her friends over the noise.

"Yes!" they all cried at once.

As the older girls headed for the stairs, Caroline glanced out the window.

"Samantha's here!" she cried. "And she's got somebody with her!"

Maria and the others rushed to the front window. They pressed their noses against the glass to get a better view.

"It looks like . . ." Lisa said.

"No . . . it couldn't be," Priscilla gasped.

"But it is!" Caroline squealed. "Samantha is walking up to *my* front door with *Rich Strout!* Hi, Samantha," she said as she opened the front door. "Come on in."

The other girls were silent. No one knew what to say to a big television star. Caroline felt the same way. What if she said something really dumb?

"This is my new cousin, Rich Strout," Samantha told everyone as if they might not recognize him.

"Wow! Rich Strout from *Harry's Grill!*" said the clown. He sounded just as impressed as the girls were.

"Oh!" Mandy White cried. "It's *Thomas!*"

The younger girls pushed their way past Caroline and her friends and stared up at the actor.

Caroline could hardly believe her eyes. What could be better than a party with Rich Strout? If her parents had allowed her to have her own party next week, Rich would probably have gone back to California. But for now, he was in Caroline's house and she just had to make him stay.

Taking a deep breath, she asked him, "Have you been to any parties lately?"

Rich glanced around the room, from the balloons and streamers to the clown, the smiling little girls, and the speechless older ones. "I can't say that I've been to any parties like *this*," he said.

Caroline grinned. "Then you're invited. It's my birthday party—and my little sister's."

"I . . ." He looked over Caroline's head. When she turned to follow his gaze, she saw that Laurie had come into the room. Laurie smiled shyly at Rich, and he suddenly said, "I think I'll accept your invitation."

Vicki grabbed Rich by the hand and told him, "Come with us. The clown's going to do magic!"

The clown trudged back to the center of the living room where he had left his supplies. All the girls found seats on the furniture or the floor. When Vicki finally released Rich's hand, he went over and stood next to Laurie.

But the poor clown was so nervous that his tricks didn't work. When he tried to pull a string of scarves out of his sleeve, they got stuck. Then he wanted to produce a quarter from behind Vicki's ear, but his hand came away empty.

"I feel sorry for him," Maria whispered to Caroline.

Caroline whispered back, "I don't blame him. I'd trip over my own feet if Rich Strout was watching me."

Rich also noticed the clown's problems. He said, "I know a little magic."

The clown nodded toward his supplies. "Help yourself." Then he and Rich changed places.

Rich waved a blue scarf in the air. Then he tucked it into his right sleeve. Next, he showed everybody a red scarf before slipping it up his left sleeve. He flashed one of his Thomas smiles, and Caroline's knees felt weak.

"You know, I get tutored on the set of *Harry's Grill* with the other kids on the show," he said. "We work hard, but we have a lot of fun. Kit, the guy who plays my friend Scooter, is so bad at science that he almost blew up the set last week."

Everyone was so interested in what he was saying that they forgot all about the scarves—until he reached back and pulled the red one, the blue one, and five others from behind his neck.

"How did you do that?" the clown wanted to know.

Rich winked at him. "I'll show you later."

He did three other tricks before he said, "That's it. I don't know any more."

"Can I have your autograph?" Patricia asked, although she was supposed to be helping her mother in the kitchen.

When Rich said, "Sure," he was mobbed. Patricia handed him a pen and passed out Snuggle Kittens napkins to Vicki and the little girls. Then he signed his name on every napkin.

"Aren't you going to get an autograph?" Susan asked Caroline.

"Maybe later, when he's not so busy," Caroline said.

"I think I'll wait, too," Diane said. "The munchkins have him surrounded."

"Rich really is nice," Samantha told Caroline. "My parents went to lunch with Uncle Stanley and Rich's mom, so I didn't have any way to get to the party until he volunteered to give me a ride."

"He's not stuck-up or anything," Wendy said. "I've got *twelve* cousins, and they were all too busy to come to our play last year. And it's not like any of them are famous, like Rich Strout."

Caroline remembered their second-grade play. All the kids in her class had been very excited about it, and she had been so proud and happy that her whole family had been there, even Grandpa Nevelson.

"I bet Rich would have come if he'd been my cousin then," Samantha said. "He'd probably have flown all the way from California."

Caroline doubted that, but she didn't want to say anything. She was perfectly happy just having him right there in her very own living room.

"Little ladies," Mrs. Zucker called, trying to get Vicki's attention, "it's time for cake and games in the kitchen."

11

THE BEST PARTY IN THE WORLD!

As Laurie herded the little girls into the next room, Mrs. Zucker approached the older ones. "And *you* ladies are cordially invited into the family room."

The six-year-olds were popping balloons as Caroline and her guests filed through the kitchen. The first thing they saw on the family room wall was a big drawing of a man's face.

"It's Mr. Fletcher!" Lisa exclaimed. Mr. Fletcher was the principal of Hart Elementary School.

"My mom drew it," Maria said proudly.

"But someone shaved off his beard," Priscilla said.

"And I've got it." Mrs. Zucker waved several brown paper beards. "We're going to play pin-the-beard-on-Mr.-Fletcher!"

Maria was the first to be blindfolded. She stuck her beard on Mr. Fletcher's nose. Priscilla put hers on his right ear.

While Caroline was waiting for her turn, she wondered where Rich had gone. Then she saw him through the doorway to the kitchen. He was helping Laurie with the little girls.

"Do you think Rich likes Laurie?" Caroline asked Samantha.

Samantha looked into the kitchen, too. She giggled. "Wouldn't that be neat?"

"What?" Maria asked.

Caroline said, "Wouldn't it be too much if Rich liked Laurie?"

"He'd visit us all the time," Samantha said with a smile.

Then it was Caroline's turn to attack Mr. Fletcher. She stuck her beard on his mouth, the closest anyone had come.

"Can I try?" Patricia asked, pouting. "Everyone's having fun except me."

Mrs. Zucker wrapped the blindfold around

Patricia's head. In seconds, she planted the beard directly on Mr. Fletcher's chin.

"Did she peek?" Priscilla wanted to know.

"Of course not," Caroline said, jumping to her sister's defense. "My sister's really smart, that's all."

The next game was a treasure hunt that took the girls all over the house. When they returned to the family room, Mrs. Zucker had set up a table in the middle of it. There was a pale pink cloth over the table, and an aqua paper plate, punch cup, and a pink-and-aqua striped party napkin at each place.

Once everyone was seated, Laurie brought in the birthday cake. She set it in front of Caroline and said, "Take a big breath."

Caroline wondered how she would ever blow out all the candles. Rich Strout was now standing next to Laurie, and just being in the same room with him made Caroline breathless.

Mrs. Zucker patted her oldest daughter on the head and said, "Make a wish, honey."

Caroline closed her eyes and sucked in as much air as her lungs could hold. Then she made her wish—that the party would never end.

Whoosh! She blew out all ten candles, nine plus one to grow on. Her friends clapped. Then Caroline cut the cake, and her mother and Laurie served cake and ice cream to everybody, even Rich Strout.

When all the girls had eaten as much as they could hold, Lisa looked at Rich shyly. "Could I have your autograph now?" she asked.

"Sure." He signed her napkin.

"Me, too!" Priscilla said, pushing her napkin toward him.

"Ooh . . ." Caroline leaped out of her chair. "I left my new pen upstairs!"

She dashed up to her room. When she came back with the pen, Maria was fluttering her eyelashes at the TV star. "Would you write 'To my special friend, Maria' on my napkin?" she asked.

"No problem." Rich grinned at Maria and all the girls sighed. Then he came over to Caroline. "Would you like an autograph, too?"

Caroline was so excited she could only nod.

Using her multi-color pen, Rich wrote in purple ink: *Happy birthday to Caroline Zucker, one of my favorite fans.* It was followed by a scribble that Caroline guessed was supposed to say *Rich Strout.*

She closed her eyes and sighed. The party was better than *anything* she and Maria could have planned. It was the best birthday party *ever*—even better than Samantha's last birthday party, when they had gone horseback riding and Samantha's horse refused to do anything except eat grass.

On Monday, no one was going to be teasing Caroline about her horrible party. Instead, anyone who hadn't been invited was going to be green with envy!

An hour later, after Caroline had opened all her presents, her friends got ready to leave.

Rich Strout held Samantha's jacket while she put it on. Then he smiled at Caroline. "Thank you for inviting me to your party. I had a very nice time. But I didn't have a present for you."

"That's all right." Caroline wanted to tell him that it had been super just having him there, but she didn't.

He shook his head. "No. I ate your cake and ice cream. I owe you something more than just my autograph. Happy birthday, Caroline." He leaned down and kissed her cheek, and everyone gasped. The whole school was going to know about the kiss on Monday, and Caroline was delighted.

After the last guest had gone and Mr. Zucker had returned, Caroline sighed happily. "I'm *never* going to wash my cheek," she said.

Her father laughed, and Patricia and Vicki giggled.

But now Caroline was serious. Taking a deep breath, she said, "Uh . . . Mom and Dad, thanks for the great party. I had a wonderful time."

Mr. and Mrs. Zucker smiled at each other. Then Mrs. Zucker gave her a big hug. "Happy birthday, Caroline. I love you."

Her father hugged her, too.

"What about me?" Vicki said, jumping up and down.

"And me?" Patricia added.

Their parents opened their arms, and everybody hugged each other.

"I have the greatest family in the world," Caroline told them all. Life was just too exciting. She never knew what was going to happen next, and she loved it that way!